A LITTLE BOOK OF flowers

RUSKIN BOND

RUPA

Published by
Rupa Publications India Pvt. Ltd 2019
7/16, Ansari Road, Daryaganj
New Delhi 110002

Sales Centres:
Allahabad Bengaluru Chennai
Hyderabad Jaipur Kathmandu
Kolkata Mumbai

Copyright © Ruskin Bond 2019

Book Illustrations by Prabhjyot Majithia
Calligraphy by Abhinandan Khanna

All rights reserved.
No part of this publication may be reproduced,
transmitted, or stored in a retrieval system, in any
form or by any means, electronic, mechanical,
photocopying, recording or otherwise, without the
prior permission of the publisher.

ISBN: 978-93-5333-371-3

First impression 2019

10 9 8 7 6 5 4 3 2 1

The moral right of the author has been asserted.

Printed at Parksons Graphics Pvt. Ltd., Mumbai

This book is sold subject to the condition that it
shall not, by way of trade or otherwise,
be lent, resold, hired out, or otherwise circulated,
without the publisher's prior consent,
in any form of binding or cover other than
that in which it is published.

Contents

Introduction / 7

The Poppy / 11

The Rose / 17

The Jasmine / 25

The Dandelion / 33

The Geranium / 41

The Crocus (Saffron) / 47

The Daisy / 55

The Marigold / 63

The Sunflower / 67

The Cosmos / 73

The Nasturtium / 81

The Buttercup / 87

The Snapdragon / 93

The Indian Pink / 99

The Zinnia / 105

The Violet / 111

The Fragrant Ones / 117

Introduction

Flowers are warm and fragrant. Almost every flower that I know, wild or cultivated, has its own unique quality, whether it be subtle fragrance or arresting colour or liveliness of design. Flowers are also one of the best things about the hills in the summer, for in winter, unfortunately, the hillsides become brown and dry—the only colour being the red sorrel growing from the limestone rocks.

But it is summer now and I'm grateful to all the marigolds and roses and buttercups and violets for making the world around me so beautiful. For several decades now I have been living in the Himalayas and I've never stopped being in awe of its beauty. It was this very beauty which prompted me to keep a little notebook on me each time I went for a walk, so that I could pen down any thoughts that came to my mind when I came across these lovely flowers. This little book on flowers comprises some of those thoughts on my favourite flowers. Here you'll read about the poppies, the snapdragons, the geraniums, the crocus, the cosmos, and many more. My publisher has also very kindly agreed to provide a few note pages between my writings, so that you can jot down your feelings and observations too when you come across these flowers or other gifts of nature.

Carry this little book with you when you travel to the hills or valleys or beaches, and if you come across a flower that inspires you, write about it. It will help you remember that feeling forever.

Ruskin Bond

The Poppy

The poppy is extravagantly beautiful although sadly short-lived. It is a classic flower, known all over the world, and praised in ancient times by poets and philosophers.

It has one great advantage over other flowers. It grows as easily in the wild as in your garden. You will find it in the cornfields of Europe as well as in the terraced stages of the Himalayas and Central Asia. Travelling in a train through France, you will find yourself passing through what appears to be lakes of blood or seas of fire as sheets of scarlet poppies spread over the fields.

The garden poppy takes many forms and colours—scarlet, white, purple, and grows best when fully exposed to sunshine, fresh air, and a dry gritty soil.

When the harvest's ended
And the fields are bare,
The poppy, red and splendid,
Is still found growing there.

· Ruskin Bond ·

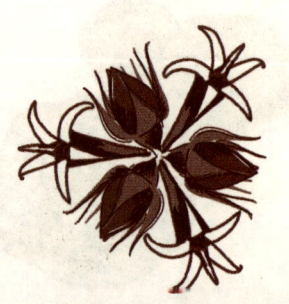

'One person's weed is another person's wildflower.'

The Rose

In the world's folklore and literature the rose stands for love and beauty.

Poets have written rapturously of the rose, one of them declaring that the rose came into existence at the same instance as the rising of Venus from the sea.

'One day,' said the Persian poet Saadi, 'I saw a rose-bush surrounded by a tuft of grass. "What!" I cried. "Does that poor plant dare to place itself in the company of roses?'" He was about to tear the grass away when it meekly addressed him, saying 'Spare me! I am not the rose, it is true; but from my perfume anyone can know that I have lived with roses.'

Roses are admired both for its beauty and fragrance, and we who love and cultivate them may rightfully called ourselves Rosarians—not to be confused with the Rotarians, although I am sure there are rose-lovers among the Rotarian fraternity.

The red rose stands for love and beauty, the white rose for

silence. White and red roses together stand for unity and warmth of the heart. You should grow them side by side.

The rosebud has its admirers too. It is given as a confession of love. 'You are young and beautiful,' is the message of the lover.

There are hundreds of varieties of roses and they can be cultivated in diverse climates. I have seen some marvelous roses in the gardens of a hot, crowded city such as Saharanpur, as well as in parks and roadside flowerbeds all over Bhutan.

· Ruskin Bond ·

'In joy or sadness, flowers are our constant friends.'

The Jasmine

The jasmine flowers grow in many parts of the world—South Africa, North America, Europe—but the Indian jasmine is special, because of its fragrance and its romantic associations.

In an old book I read that when someone gives you a garland or necklace of jasmine, the giver is saying, 'I attach myself to you.'

Leafing through an old dairy that I kept when I was young and in love, I found these lines that I had written for a beautiful friend:

Jasmine flowers in her hair,
Languid summer days are here,
And sweet longing scents the air.

The white star-shaped secretly scented flowers are particularly suited to the complexions of our southern beauties.

Apart from the rose, no other flower has been so celebrated

in literature and folklore. Many insects are attracted by the rare fragrance of its flowers. 'Jasmine is sweet, and has many loves,' said Tom Hood in his poem 'Flowers'.

'Happiness radiates like the fragrance from a flower and draws all good things towards you.'

The Dandelion

Dandelions will pop up in the most unexpected places—but not where you plant them. They are nature's rebels, who will shun your garden but grow on your steps.

I found my well-meaning neighbour trying to remove a dandelion from my steps. 'It's just a weed,' she said.

'Not so,' I told her, and

showed her the white milk oozing from its stem, a sure healer of warts and other skin growths.

Dandelion is French for lion's tooth, the name referring to the tooth-like leaves; but I prefer to think of its golden flower and flaunting seed-ball as being truly lion-like.

The dandelion opens its petals to the first rays of the sun and closes when the sunlight fades. It is called Love's Oracle because of the custom of blowing on its puffball of seeds to discover whether 'she loves me' or 'she loves me not'.

· Ruskin Bond ·

'Well, it's gone now,' said my neighbour. 'I've pulled it out.'

'No, you haven't,' I said.

'It will grow again.' And I recited the song of the Dandelion fairy:

'...Sillies, what are you about,
With your shapes and hoes of iron?
You can never drive me out—
Me, the dauntless Dandelion!'

"Pick a flower on earth and you move the farthest star."

The Geranium

I have always kept a geranium—preferably a scarlet or blood-red geranium—on the table beside my sunny window.

If I feel low in spirits I have only to look at it and its bright colours bring me to life again. I call it my flower of hope and optimism.

There are many kinds of geraniums and the flowers

come in many shades and colours. They like plenty of sun and moisture but not dry heat. I have seen magnificent geraniums in Bangalore and in our hill stations, but they struggle to grow in Delhi!

A wild geranium flower in the hills in October; a pretty bright blue flower on a trailing stem; but it won't transfer to a garden.

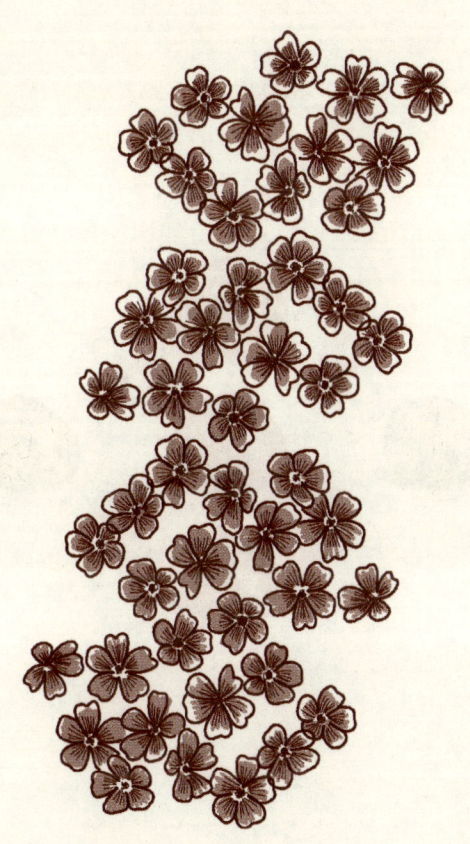

'Just living is not enough... one must have sunshine, freedom, and a little flower.',

The Crocus (Saffron)

The name comes from the Greek 'crocus', meaning saffron.

A certain young gentleman named Crocus went to play coits[1] in a field with Mercury, and Mercury's coit accidentally hit him on the head. The coit

---

[1] Modern spelling: Quoits

killed him, and saffron sprang from the ground where he had bled, and was called crocus in commemoration of the event.

Well, it's a nice story!

There are many species of crocus; some are pastel-blue with orange-yellow throats; others are violet with long sweet-scented tubes. The dried stigmas of the latter constitute the genuine saffron of commerce. The finest crocuses, found in our part of the world, are known to traders as 'cloth of gold'.

There are many tales and legends connected with the

crocus. One of them tells us that the word crocodile means crocus-dreader, and that the reptile dreads this plant. It is only when the crocodile is taken to a place where the crocus grows that its tears are genuine!

And historians tell us that Roman ladies dyed their hair with saffron, though priests warned them that the flame-like colour presaged the fires of Hell! This did not stop the ladies from using it.

'A pound of saffron is worth a pound of money,' goes an old saying. And that is still true of it today.

· Ruskin Bond ·

'Every flower is a soul blossoming in nature.'

The Daisy

The poet Burns called the daisy a 'Wee, modest, flower', but the daisy is not modest. It will find its own space and spread itself like a snow-white, pink-tipped carpet along the ground. How could it be modest when we have named it daisy, meaning 'eye of the day'?

A couple of summers ago—it was early May—driving from the

Yamuna Bridge to Chakrata, the road was bordered by large white daisies for the entire distance. I could understand why this simple but striking flower had inspired so many poets, including Wordsworth, who couldn't stop writing about it.

There are large daisies and there are small daisies, and the latter, embedded in the retaining wall near my home, are in flower as I write. Children pluck them to make daisy chains.

The flowers are open during the day, closing their petals at the sunset hour. But they will

be up with the sun and ready to play all-day long on a bright and cheerful day.

In the early years of the last century Daisy was a popular name for girls. My mother would often sing a popular music hall song, and I remember it perfectly:

'Daisy, Daisy,
I'm half-crazy
All for the love of you.
I won't be a stylish marriage
Cause I can't afford a carriage,
But you'll look sweet
Upon the seat
Of a bicycle built for two!'

'The Earth laughs in the flowers.'

'A flower cannot blossom without sunshine and a man cannot live without love.'

The Marigold

How can I ignore the marigold that is so much a part of our lives in India?

Garlands of marigold. Temple offerings. Marriages.

There are those simple Indian marigolds that appear to look after themselves. And then there are the garden marigolds—the big Africans, the delicate French. The calendula also belongs to the marigold family.

These hardy, colourful blooms make a great show, either on their own or en masse.

'As dependable as a marigold,' my grandmother used to say.

And true enough, they never let you down.

The Sunflower

As a child I liked wandering among tall flowering plants like sunflowers, cosmos, and hollyhocks. They were so much taller them me! Now we are almost at the same level, and I can go eye to eye with the sunflower, so generous with its life-giving seeds.

On a visit to Bhutan last year, we drove down roads

lined with sunflowers. It was late September and everything was in flower, a country blessed with gardens and orchards.

A field of life-giving sunflowers is an awe-inspiring sight, bringing a childhood song back to me:

> *Just like a sunflower*
> *After a sunshower,*
> *My inspiration is you.'*

· Ruskin Bond ·

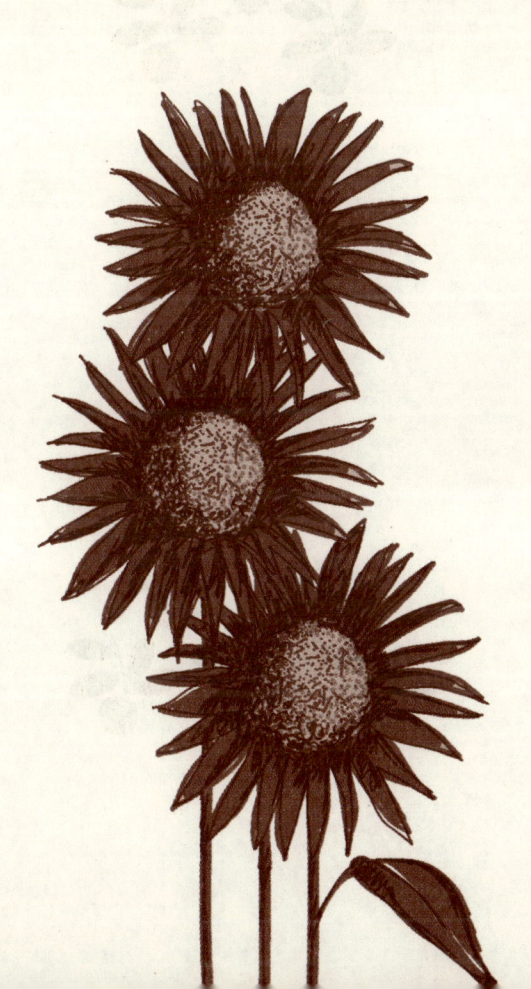

'You can cut all the flowers but cannot keep spring from coming.'

The Cosmos

Cosmos means the universe.

Well, if you can see the world in a grain of sand, surely you can see the universe in the cosmos flower.

This radiant, cheerful flower has always been one of my favourites. There was a time when the open spaces in and around Mussoorie and other hill stations were ablaze with the fresh-faced cosmos in dense clusters. They were, in fact, a feature of the hill station. Now, sadly, I cannot find a single cosmos, in a garden or on the hillside. This disappearance is a mystery to me. Is it due to climate change or the hyper-activity of the builders? Concrete has been taking over from grass, and as a result many beautiful plants are disappearing.

Some compensation came my way last year, when on a visit to Shillong and Cherrapunji, I found cosmos flowering on the hillsides in small village gardens.

· Ruskin Bond ·

The cosmos needs space in which to flourish. It will make a great show on a hillside or a sunny corner of the own, and once established it will look after itself.

'A flower dosen't hate you or love you, it just exists.'

'Happiness held is the seed;
Happiness shared is the flower.'

The Nasturtium

The nasturtium also looks after itself once it has found a homely corner of the garden. It will also dwell on a trellis or an old wall. During the monsoon the foliage gets quite dense, and then the flowers—orange or yellow or bright red—look out from their leafy cover like the Lone Ranger on his steed.

My grandmother used to put

nasturtium leaves in salads and sandwiches. She said they were good for the heart, and they might well have been, as she lived to a good old age. The seeds of the nasturtium are as pungent as chili—they will make an interesting addition to a mixed pickle!

'Let us dance in the Sun, wearing wild flowers in our head.'

The Buttercup

Common to the Himalayan foothills, as well as to the English countryside, bright-yellow buttercups spring up in the summer grass and are among the first flowers (along with daisies) to become familiar to children.

In flower lore, the buttercup stands for cheerfulness, and in cold climates it is the true harbinger of summer.

Clutching buttercups, the children dance and sing:

'Oh little playmates when I love,
The sky is summer-blue
And meadows full of buttercups
Are spread abroad for you.'

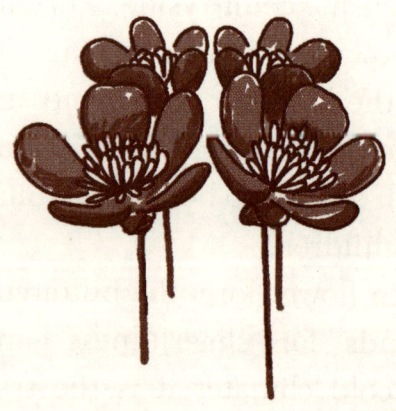

· Ruskin Bond ·

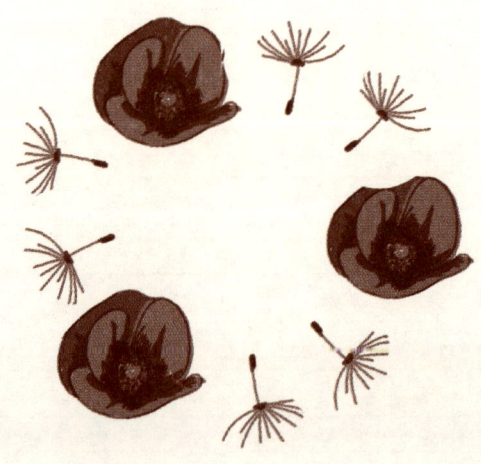

'A flower blossoms for its own joy.'

The Snapdragon

I wonder why the early botanists chose ugly names for flowers, such as the unpronounceable antirrhinum for this popular garden flower, better known as the snapdragon.

As a child I loved pinching the flower's moist mouths, to open and close them, saying *Snap-dragon* or *Doggy* or *Bunny-nose*!

Snapdragons have many colours and make a great show in the garden, attracting bees and other insects who also like to get between those alluring lips. This subtle fragrance drifts across the lawn.

No garden is complete without some friendly snap-dragons in residence.

'If you have a garden and a library, you have everything you need.'

The Indian Pink

The Indian pink keeps flowering
without end,
Sturdy and modest,
A loyal friend.

So I wrote in an old notebook, and I am still attached to this little friend, a relative of the more showy carnation.

There are many varieties of pink—carnation pinks, double pinks, variegated pinks—and their common characteristic is their highly attractive scent.

The word 'pink' has a variety of meanings. We talk of 'the pink of perfection', of being in the 'pink of health'. The little finger is also called a 'pinky'. But a flower does not cease to be pink though its colour may be white, purple or yellow.

'Stretching his hands up to reach the stars, too often man forgets the flowers at his feet.'

The Zinnia

The zinnia is a generous flower. Cut one bloom and two will take its place. It comes in many bright colours, bringing the garden to life on the dandiest of days. And their old-fashioned pastel shades make a great show indoors, in a bowl or vase. It is a hardy plant and will look after itself once it is established in a flowerbed.

The early Aztecs honoured the flower for its beauty, and we are told that Cortés the Spanish conquistador, found it flushing in the legendary gardens of Montezuma when he captured the city of Mexico.

It was named after the German botanist and physician Johann Zinn, a pioneer brain specialist who gave his name to a part of the brain still known as the Zonule of Zinn.

In plant lore, the Zinnia stands for 'thought of absent friends'.

"I always like to have flowers on the table. I think they make it look special."

The Violet

Up here in the Himalayan foothills I know when its springtime—the first flowers appear on the hillslopes, and these early flowers are the modest violets, making their way through wild clover. They come in shades of lavender or blue or purple, their little heart-shaped leaves turning up in gardens and on the hillside, their violet nectar attracting bccs and butterflies.

The Persians loved violets. It was also the flower of Athens, in Ancient Greece. The Romans used violets in medicines and love philtres. For American Indians it was a symbol of love and courage. When the first English colonists arrived in America they were delighted to find violets growing in the wild, for as children they had picked them in English meadows.

'Sweet Violet, I think of you
When I am low and
feeling blue...'

· Ruskin Bond ·

African violets are easy to grow indoors and will flower throughout the year.

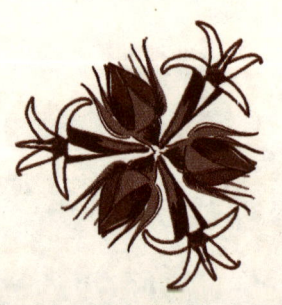

'Flowers
are a proud
assertion that
a vein of beauty
outvalued
all the utilities
of the World.'

The Fragrant Ones

One spring I went in search of sweet peas. I was missing their extravagant fragrance. But no one seemed to be growing them; too much trouble perhaps. They need good soil, and they need to be trained and supported; they need something to climb.

In short, they need a full-time gardener!

It was sometime in March that I visited the Delhi University gardens. There I found masses of sweet peas. I was intoxicated by their fragrance, their colours, and their extravagance. I am sure the students appreciated them too. Well, some of them did at least I hope.

The Calamondin Orange is a delightful little flowering plant, which produces sweetly seated flowers and pretty dwarf oranges. It needs plenty of light, even hot sunshine, and will do

well both indoors or out in the garden where it will grow into a small tree. But its fruit is strictly for the birds!

'By plucking the petals you do not gather the beauty of the flower.'

'Life is the flower for which Love is the honey.'